A LONG TIME AGO, IN A GALAXY FAR, FAR AWAY....

Meet the CHARACTERS

OBI-WAN KENOBI

Many believe Ben Kenobi is just an **old crazy wizard**, but in truth he's a **Jedi Knight**, a great warrior of the **Old Republic** who now lives in the desert wasteland of Tatooine.

LUKE SKYWALKER

Luke is a young farmer who lives on the remote **planet Tatooine** with his **Uncle Owen** and his **Aunt Beru**. He dreams of becoming a **space pilot** and living a life of adventure: a mysterious message will change his life forever, revealing his true destiny.

PRINCESS LEIA ORGANA

Strong-willed and **brave**, Leia Organa of Alderaan is part of the **Galactic Senate**. She hates the Empire: she travels on her consular ship to deliver secret messages for the Rebellion.

C-3PO & R2-D2

C-3PO is a **loyal protocol droid** – fluent in over six million forms of communication. His life would not be the same without his resolute counterpart, the small R2-D2 – a **resourceful astromech droid**.

HAN SOLO & CHEWBACCA

Reckless, **daring** but sometimes **overly confident**, Han Solo is a **mercenary pirate** and a **smuggler**, captain of the ***Millennium Falcon***. His first mate is Chewbacca: a **Wookiee**, an expert **mechanic** and Han's best friend.

Meet the CHARACTERS

DARTH VADER

Darth Vader is a **Dark Lord of the Sith**, a very powerful master of the **dark side of the Force**. Unnerving and dangerous, he commands the **Imperial fleet** and rules his forces through terror.

GRAND MOFF TARKIN

Grand Moff Tarkin is **Governor of the Imperial Outland Regions** and **commander** of the horrific **Death Star superweapon**. Ambitious and ruthless, he carries out the orders of the Emperor.

STORMTROOPERS

Highly trained soldiers, the stormtroopers maintain order throughout the galaxy with ruthless efficiency. Equipped with the finest weapons, they are the **elite troops** of the **Galactic Empire**.

GREEDO

Greedo is a **Rodian bounty hunter**. He works for the repellent crime lord **Jabba the Hutt** and he is trying to locate and capture Han Solo for him – Han is guilty of losing Hutt's cargo.

TUSKEN RAIDERS

Savage and violent, the Tusken Raiders – also known as **Sand People** – are a great danger of the **Jundland Wastes** on Tatooine. Covered in tattered rags and robes, they survive where no one else can.

Episode IV

A NEW HOPE

It is a period of civil war. Rebel spaceships, striking from a hidden base, have won their first victory against the evil Galactic Empire.

During the battle, Rebel spies managed to steal secret plans to the Empire's ultimate weapon, the DEATH STAR, an armored space station with enough power to destroy an entire planet.

Pursued by the Empire's sinister agents, Princess Leia races home aboard her starship, custodian of the stolen plans that can save her people and restore freedom to the galaxy....

TATOOINE SYSTEM: A REBEL STARSHIP IS PURSUED BY THE EMPIRE.

BOOM

FSHHHH-BOOM

PEW
PEW
PEW

PEW
PEW
RETREAT!
PEW

TEAR THIS SHIP APART UNTIL *YOU'VE* FOUND THOSE *PLANS* AND BRING ME THE PASSENGERS.
I WANT THEM *ALIVE*.

IN ANOTHER SECTION OF THE SHIP...
•••

R2-D2, WHERE ARE YOU?

WHERE HAVE YOU BEEN? THEY ARE HEADING IN THIS DIRECTION.

THERE'S ONE. SET FOR *STUN.*

PEW

FZEEEW

SHE'LL BE ALL RIGHT. INFORM **LORD VADER** WE HAVE A PRISONER.

WHERE ARE YOU GOING?
●●●!
SECRET MISSION? WHAT PLANS? WHAT ARE YOU TALKING ABOUT?

I'M GOING TO REGRET THIS.

A FEW MOMENTS LATER.
LORD VADER, ONLY YOU COULD BE SO BOLD...
DON'T ACT SO SURPRISED, *YOUR HIGHNESS.* SEVERAL TRANSMISSIONS WERE BEAMED TO THIS SHIP BY *REBEL SPIES.* I WANT TO KNOW WHAT HAPPENED TO THE PLANS.

I DON'T KNOW WHAT YOU'RE TALKING ABOUT. I'M A MEMBER OF THE IMPERIAL SENATE ON A *DIPLOMATIC MISSION* TO ALDERAAN...
YOU ARE PART OF THE REBEL ALLIANCE AND *A TRAITOR.*

TAKE HER AWAY!
LORD VADER?

THE BATTLE STATION PLANS ARE NOT ABOARD THIS SHIP. AN *ESCAPE POD* WAS JETTISONED DURING THE FIGHTING, BUT NO LIFE FORMS WERE ABOARD.

SHE MUST HAVE HIDDEN THE PLANS IN THE ESCAPE POD.

SEND A DETACHMENT DOWN TO *RETRIEVE THEM.*

TATOOINE DESERT.
HOW DID WE GET INTO THIS MESS?

WHERE ARE YOU GOING? I'M NOT GOING THAT WAY. IT'S MUCH *TOO ROCKY.*

●●●!
WHAT MISSION? WHAT ARE YOU TALKING ABOUT?

I'VE HAD JUST ABOUT ***ENOUGH*** OF YOU! GO THAT WAY! YOU'LL BE MAL-FUNCTIONING WITHIN A DAY!

●●●
AND DON'T LET ME CATCH YOU FOLLOWING ME BEGGING FOR HELP, BECAUSE YOU WON'T GET IT!

A *TRANSPORT!* I'M SAVED! OVER HERE! HELP!

TATOOINE, ROCK CANYON. LATER.

SHOOTOGAWA!
ZZAAKTT

BAM

THEEK.
IBANA.
IBANA.

R2-D2! IT IS YOU! IT IS YOU!

THE NEXT DAY.
SOMEONE WAS IN THE POD. THE TRACKS GO OFF IN THIS DIRECTION.
LOOK SIR...
...DROIDS!

WE STOPPED. WAKE UP! WAKE UP!
●●●!

TATOOINE DESERT. LARS HOMESTEAD.

LUKE!

LUKE, TELL UNCLE IF HE GETS A *TRANSLATOR*, BE SURE IT SPEAKS BOCCE.
IT LOOKS LIKE WE DON'T HAVE MUCH OF A CHOICE...

"...BUT I'LL REMIND HIM."
OF COURSE I CAN SPEAK BOCCE, SIR. IT'S LIKE A SECOND LANGUAGE FOR ME.

I'LL TAKE THIS ONE TOO.

LUKE, TAKE THESE TWO OVER TO THE GARAGE, I WANT YOU TO HAVE BOTH OF THEM CLEANED UP BEFORE DINNER.

BUT I WAS GOING INTO TOSCHE STATION TO PICK UP SOME POWER CONVERTERS...
YOU CAN WASTE TIME WITH YOUR FRIENDS WHEN YOUR CHORES ARE DONE.

ALL RIGHT, COME ON.

LARS HOMESTEAD, GARAGE AREA. LATER.
IT JUST ISN'T FAIR. BIGGS IS RIGHT. I'M NEVER GONNA GET OUT OF HERE!

IS THERE ANYTHING I MIGHT DO TO HELP?
NOT UNLESS YOU CAN ALTER TIME, SPEED UP THE HARVEST, OR TELEPORT ME *OFF THIS ROCK!*
I DON'T THINK SO, SIR.

YOU CAN CALL ME LUKE.
I AM *C-3PO*, HUMAN-CYBORG RELATIONS. AND THAT IS MY COUNTERPART, *R2-D2*.

HELLO.

YOU GOT A LOT OF CARBON SCORING HERE. IT LOOKS LIKE YOU BOYS HAVE SEEN A LOT OF *ACTION.*

YOU GOT SOMETHING JAMMED IN HERE REAL GOOD...

SNAP

BZZZ

HELP ME, OBI-WAN KENOBI. YOU'RE MY ONLY HOPE.
WHO IS SHE?

IS THERE MORE TO THIS RECORDING?
●●●!

I THINK THAT R2 UNIT WE BOUGHT MIGHT HAVE BEEN **STOLEN.** HE SAYS HE BELONGS TO SOMEONE CALLED OBI-WAN KENOBI.
I THOUGHT HE MIGHT HAVE MEANT BEN.

THAT OLD MAN'S JUST A ***CRAZY WIZARD.*** TOMORROW I WANT YOU TO TAKE THAT R2 UNIT INTO ANCHORHEAD AND HAVE ITS MEMORY ***FLUSHED.***

WHAT IF THIS OBI-WAN COMES LOOKING FOR HIM?
HE WON'T. HE ***DIED*** ABOUT THE SAME TIME AS YOUR FATHER.

HE KNEW ***MY FATHER?***

I TOLD YOU TO FORGET IT. YOUR ONLY CONCERN IS TO PREPARE THE NEW DROIDS FOR TOMORROW.
YES, SIR.

WHAT ARE YOU DOING HIDING BACK THERE?

IT WASN'T *MY FAULT*, SIR! I TOLD HIM NOT TO GO, BUT HE KEPT BABBLING ON ABOUT HIS MISSION!
OH NO...

HE'S NOWHERE IN SIGHT. BLAST IT!

PARDON ME, SIR, BUT COULDN'T WE GO AFTER HIM?
IT'S TOO DANGEROUS WITH ALL THE *SAND PEOPLE* AROUND.

"WE'LL HAVE TO WAIT UNTIL MORNING..."
THERE'S A DROID ON THE SCANNER. IT MIGHT BE OUR LITTLE R2 UNIT.

HEY! JUST WHERE DO YOU THINK YOU'RE GOING?
•••!
WHAT'S WRONG WITH HIM?

THERE ARE *SEVERAL CREATURES* APPROACHING FROM THE SOUTHEAST.
SAND PEOPLE... OR WORSE!

THEY'RE SAND PEOPLE ALL RIGHT.

I CAN SEE ONE OF...

URRAK! URRAK!

A FEW MOMENTS LATER...
!

KHEEEEE
!

?

HELLO THERE.
COME HERE, MY LITTLE FRIEND. DON'T WORRY...

"...HE'LL BE ALL RIGHT."
BEN? *BEN KENOBI!* BOY, AM I GLAD TO SEE YOU!

TELL ME, YOUNG LUKE, WHAT BRINGS YOU OUT THIS FAR?
OH, THIS LITTLE DROID! I THINK HE'S SEARCHING FOR HIS FORMER MASTER...

!
HE CLAIMS TO BE THE PROPERTY OF AN OBI-WAN KENOBI.

OBI-WAN KENOBI... NOW, THAT'S A NAME I HAVEN'T HEARD IN A *LONG TIME.*
YOU KNOW HIM?

WELL OF COURSE I KNOW HIM. HE'S *ME!*
I HAVEN'T GONE BY THE NAME OBI-WAN SINCE BEFORE YOU WERE BORN...

KENOBI'S DWELLING, LATER...
MY FATHER DIDN'T FIGHT IN THE WARS, HE WAS A NAVIGATOR ON A SPICE FREIGHTER.

THAT'S WHAT YOUR UNCLE TOLD YOU. HE DIDN'T HOLD WITH YOUR FATHER'S IDEALS.
YOU FOUGHT IN THE *CLONE WARS?*

YES. I WAS ONCE A *JEDI KNIGHT* THE SAME AS YOUR FATHER.
HE WAS THE BEST STAR-PILOT IN THE GALAXY, AND A CUNNING WARRIOR.

WHICH REMINDS ME... I HAVE SOMETHING HERE FOR YOU.

YOUR FATHER'S *LIGHTSABER.* THIS IS THE WEAPON OF A JEDI KNIGHT.
YOUR FATHER WANTED YOU TO HAVE THIS, BUT YOUR UNCLE WOULDN'T ALLOW IT.

ZMMM
FOR OVER A THOUSAND GENERATIONS THE JEDI KNIGHTS WERE THE GUARDIANS OF *PEACE* AND *JUSTICE* IN THE OLD REPUBLIC.
BEFORE THE DARK TIMES, BEFORE THE EMPIRE.

HOW DID MY FATHER DIE?
A YOUNG JEDI NAMED DARTH VADER HELPED THE EMPIRE HUNT DOWN AND *DESTROY* THE JEDI KNIGHTS.

HE BETRAYED AND MURDERED YOUR FATHER.

VADER WAS SEDUCED BY THE *DARK SIDE* OF THE *FORCE*.
THE FORCE?

THE FORCE IS WHAT GIVES THE JEDI HIS POWER. IT'S AN *ENERGY FIELD* CREATED BY ALL LIVING THINGS. IT SURROUNDS US AND PENETRATES US.

●●●!
?

THE MESSAGE!
GENERAL KENOBI, YEARS AGO YOU SERVED MY FATHER IN THE CLONE WARS. NOW HE BEGS YOU TO HELP HIM IN HIS STRUGGLE AGAINST THE EMPIRE.

I HAVE PLACED INFORMATION VITAL TO THE SURVIVAL OF THE REBELLION INTO THE MEMORY SYSTEMS OF THIS R2 UNIT.

HELP ME, OBI-WAN KENOBI, YOU'RE MY ONLY HOPE.

YOU MUST LEARN THE WAYS OF THE FORCE IF YOU'RE TO COME WITH ME TO *ALDERAAN.*
ALDERAAN? I'M NOT GOING TO ALDERAAN! I'VE GOT TO GO *HOME!*

I NEED YOUR HELP, LUKE. *SHE* NEEDS YOUR HELP.
I'M GETTING TOO OLD FOR THIS SORT OF THING.

I CAN'T GET *INVOLVED!* I'VE GOT WORK TO DO! LOOK, I CAN TAKE YOU AS FAR AS ANCHORHEAD. YOU CAN GET A TRANSPORT THERE TO MOS EISLEY.

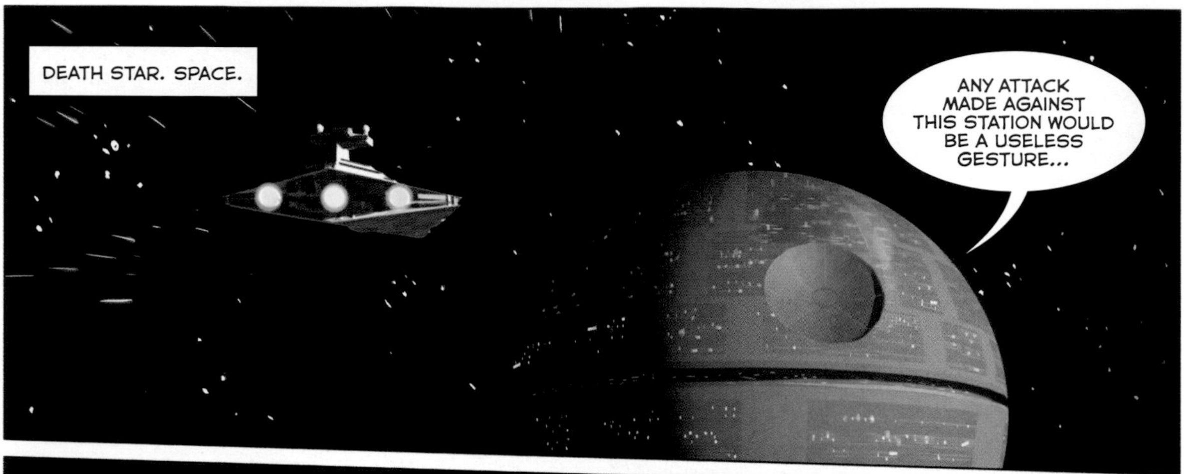
DEATH STAR. SPACE.
ANY ATTACK MADE AGAINST THIS STATION WOULD BE A USELESS GESTURE...

THIS STATION IS NOW THE ULTIMATE POWER IN THE UNIVERSE!

THE ABILITY TO DESTROY A PLANET IS INSIGNIFICANT NEXT TO THE POWER OF THE FORCE.

DON'T TRY TO FRIGHTEN US, LORD VADER. YOUR SAD DEVOTION TO THAT ANCIENT RELIGION HAS NOT HELPED YOU CONJURE UP THE STOLEN DATA TAPES...
...OR GIVEN YOU CLAIRVOYANCE ENOUGH TO FIND THE REBELS' HIDDEN FORT.

I FIND YOUR LACK OF FAITH DISTURBING.

UHHH!
ENOUGH OF THIS! VADER, RELEASE HIM!
AS YOU WISH, GOVERNOR TARKIN.
THIS BICKERING IS POINTLESS. LORD VADER WILL PROVIDE US WITH THE LOCATION OF THE REBEL FORTRESS BY THE TIME THIS STATION IS OPERATIONAL.
...

"WE WILL THEN CRUSH THE REBELLION WITH ONE SWIFT STROKE."
ONLY IMPERIAL STORMTROOPERS ARE SO PRECISE.
IF THEY TRACED THE ROBOTS HERE, THEY MAY HAVE LEARNED WHO THEY SOLD THEM TO.

AND THAT WOULD LEAD THEM...

"...BACK HOME!"

UNCLE OWEN! AUNT BERU!

OH NO...

DEATH STAR. DETENTION SECURITY AREA.

AND NOW, YOUR HIGHNESS, WE WILL *DISCUSS* THE LOCATION OF YOUR HIDDEN REBEL BASE.

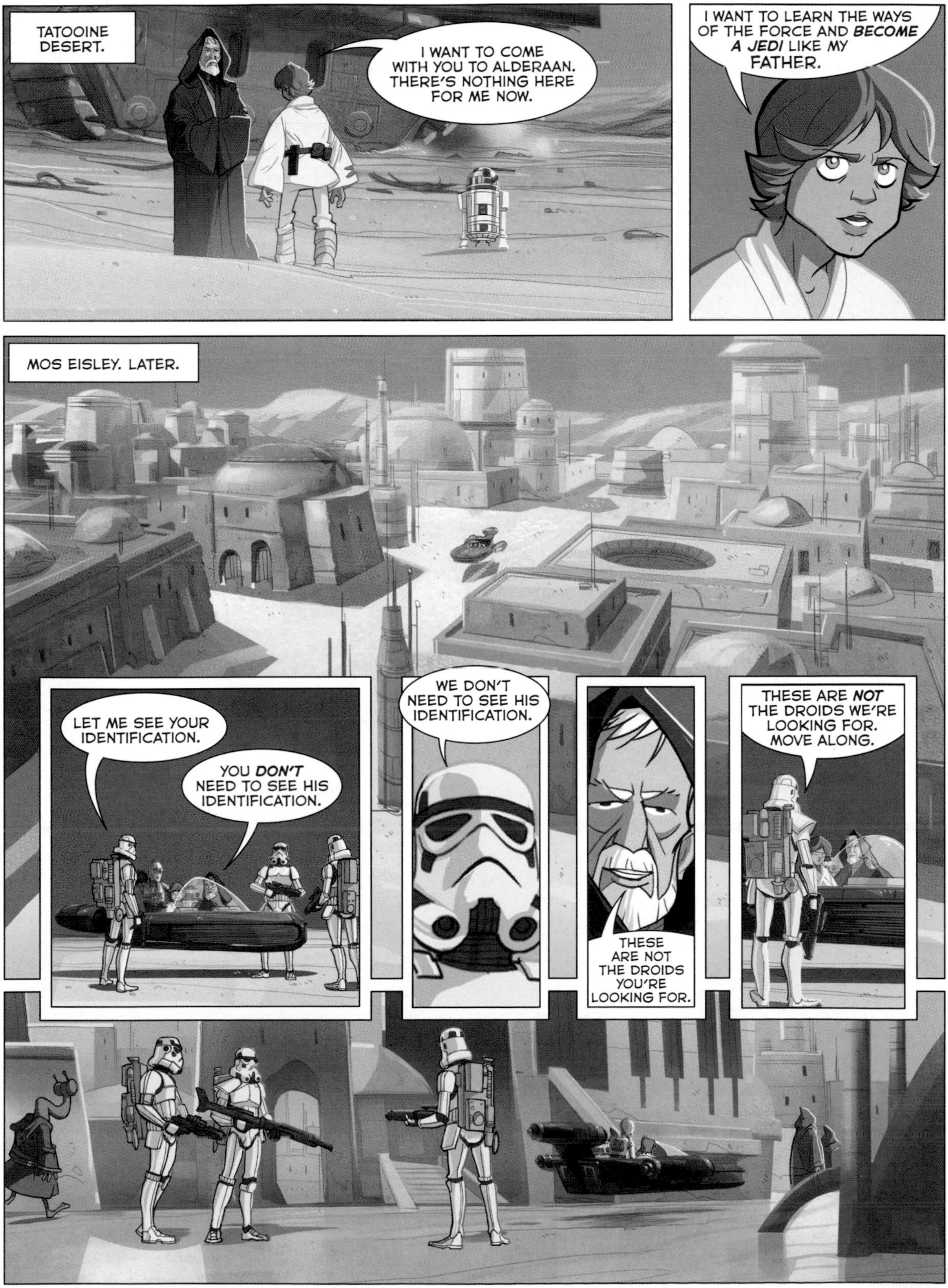

MOS EISLEY. LATER.

LET ME SEE YOUR IDENTIFICATION.

YOU ***DON'T*** NEED TO SEE HIS IDENTIFICATION.

WE DON'T NEED TO SEE HIS IDENTIFICATION.

THESE ARE NOT THE DROIDS YOU'RE LOOKING FOR.

THESE ARE ***NOT*** THE DROIDS WE'RE LOOKING FOR. MOVE ALONG.

I CAN'T UNDERSTAND HOW WE GOT BY THOSE TROOPERS.
THE FORCE CAN HAVE A STRONG INFLUENCE ON THE WEAKMINDED.

DO YOU REALLY THINK WE'RE GOING TO FIND A *PILOT*?
MOST OF THE BEST FREIGHTER PILOTS CAN BE FOUND HERE.

HAN SOLO. I'M CAPTAIN OF THE ***MILLENNIUM FALCON.***
CHEWIE HERE TELLS ME YOU'RE LOOKING FOR PASSAGE TO THE ALDERAAN SYSTEM.
YES, INDEED. IF IT'S A FAST SHIP.

FAST SHIP? I'VE *OUTRUN* IMPERIAL STARSHIPS!
WHAT'S THE CARGO?

MYSELF, THE BOY, TWO DROIDS, AND NO QUESTIONS ASKED. WE'D LIKE TO AVOID ANY IMPERIAL ENTANGLEMENTS.

WELL, IT'S GONNA COST YOU SOMETHING *EXTRA.* TEN THOUSAND, ALL IN ADVANCE.
TEN THOUSAND? WE COULD ALMOST BUY OUR OWN SHIP FOR THAT!

BUT WHO'S GOING TO FLY IT, *KID!* YOU?

YOU BET I COULD. I'M NOT SUCH A BAD PILOT MYSELF!
WE CAN PAY YOU TWO THOUSAND NOW, PLUS FIFTEEN WHEN WE REACH ALDERAAN.

SEVENTEEN? *OKAY.* YOU GUYS GOT YOURSELF A SHIP.
WE'LL LEAVE AS SOON AS YOU'RE READY. DOCKING BAY 94.

SEVENTEEN THOUSAND! THIS COULD REALLY SAVE MY NECK.
GET BACK TO THE SHIP AND GET HER READY.

GOING SOMEWHERE, SOLO?

YES, GREEDO. AS A MATTER OF FACT, I WAS JUST GOING TO SEE YOUR BOSS. TELL JABBA THAT I'VE GOT HIS MONEY.
IT'S TOO LATE.

JABBA'S THROUGH WITH YOU. HE HAS NO TIME FOR SMUGGLERS WHO DROP THEIR SHIPMENTS AT THE FIRST SIGN OF AN IMPERIAL CRUISER.

EVEN I GET BOARDED SOMETIMES. DO YOU THINK I HAD A CHOICE?
YOU CAN TELL THAT TO JABBA. HE MAY ONLY TAKE YOUR SHIP.
OVER MY DEAD BODY.

PEW
PEW

SORRY ABOUT THE *MESS*.

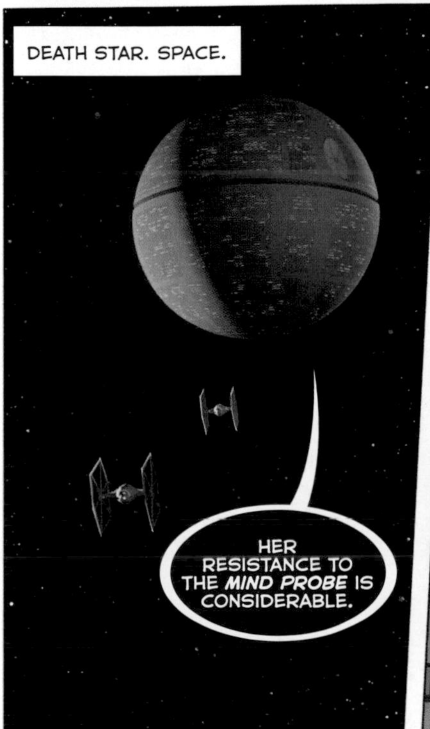
DEATH STAR. SPACE.
HER RESISTANCE TO THE *MIND PROBE* IS CONSIDERABLE.

PERHAPS SHE WOULD RESPOND TO AN ALTERNATIVE FORM OF PERSUASION.

I THINK IT IS TIME WE DEMONSTRATED THE *FULL POWER* OF THIS STATION.
SET YOUR COURSE FOR PRINCESS LEIA'S HOME PLANET OF ALDERAAN.

MOS EISLEY, DOCKING BAY 94.

WHAT A PIECE OF JUNK!

SHE'LL MAKE POINT FIVE PAST LIGHTSPEED. SHE MAY NOT LOOK LIKE MUCH, BUT SHE'S GOT IT ***WHERE IT COUNTS***, KID.
BUT WE'RE A LITTLE ***RUSHED***, SO IF YOU'LL HURRY ABOARD...

STOP THAT SHIP!
PEW
PEW
PEW
CHEWIE, GET US OUT OF HERE!
PEW

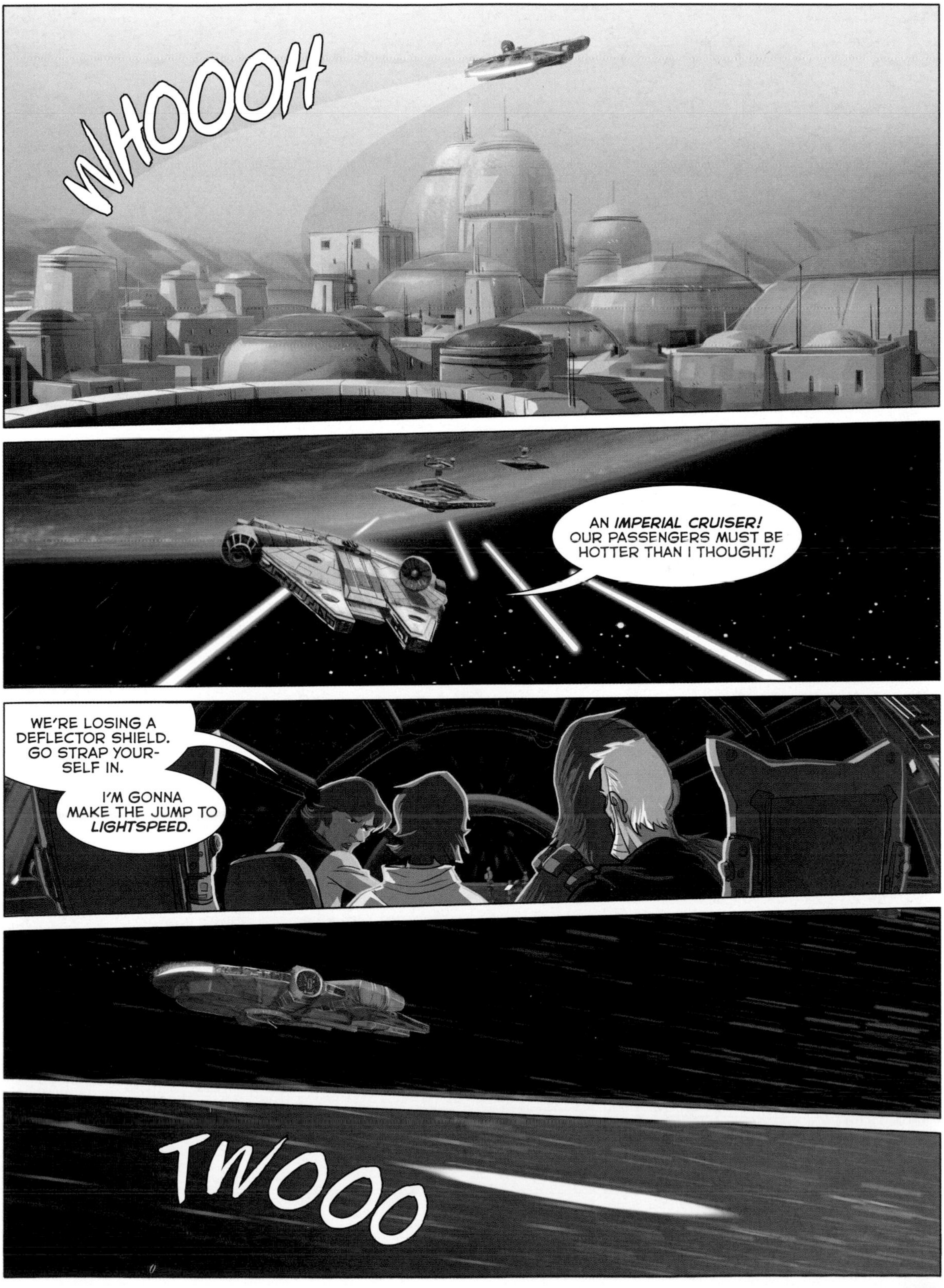

WHOOOH

TWOOO

ALDERAAN SYSTEM.
PRINCESS LEIA...
SINCE YOU ARE RELUCTANT TO PROVIDE US WITH THE LOCATION OF THE REBEL BASE, I HAVE CHOSEN TO TEST THIS STATION'S DESTRUCTIVE POWER...

...ON *YOUR* ***HOME PLANET*** OF ALDERAAN.
NO! ALDERAAN IS PEACEFUL, WE HAVE NO WEAPONS!

YOU WOULD PREFER ANOTHER TARGET? A MILITARY TARGET? THEN ***NAME THE SYSTEM!***

I GROW ***TIRED*** OF ASKING THIS.

DANTOOINE.
THEY'RE ON DANTOOINE.

YOU SEE, LORD VADER, SHE CAN BE REASONABLE.
CONTINUE WITH THE OPERATION. YOU MAY *FIRE* WHEN READY.
WHAT?

YOU'RE FAR TOO *TRUSTING.* DANTOOINE IS TOO REMOTE, BUT DON'T WORRY...

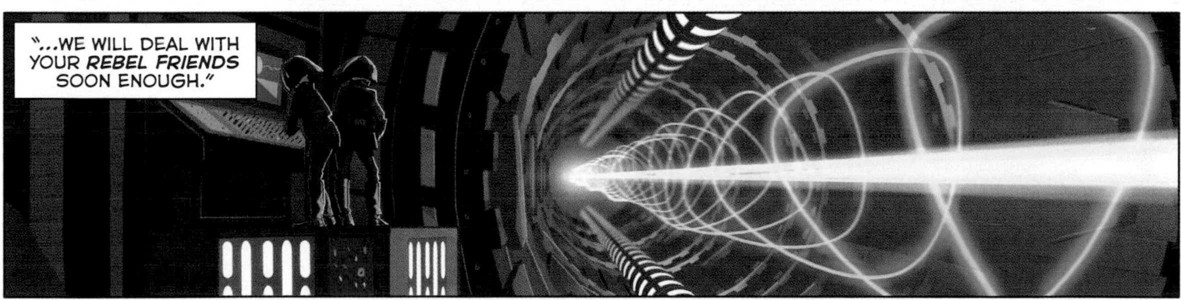
"...WE WILL DEAL WITH YOUR *REBEL FRIENDS* SOON ENOUGH."

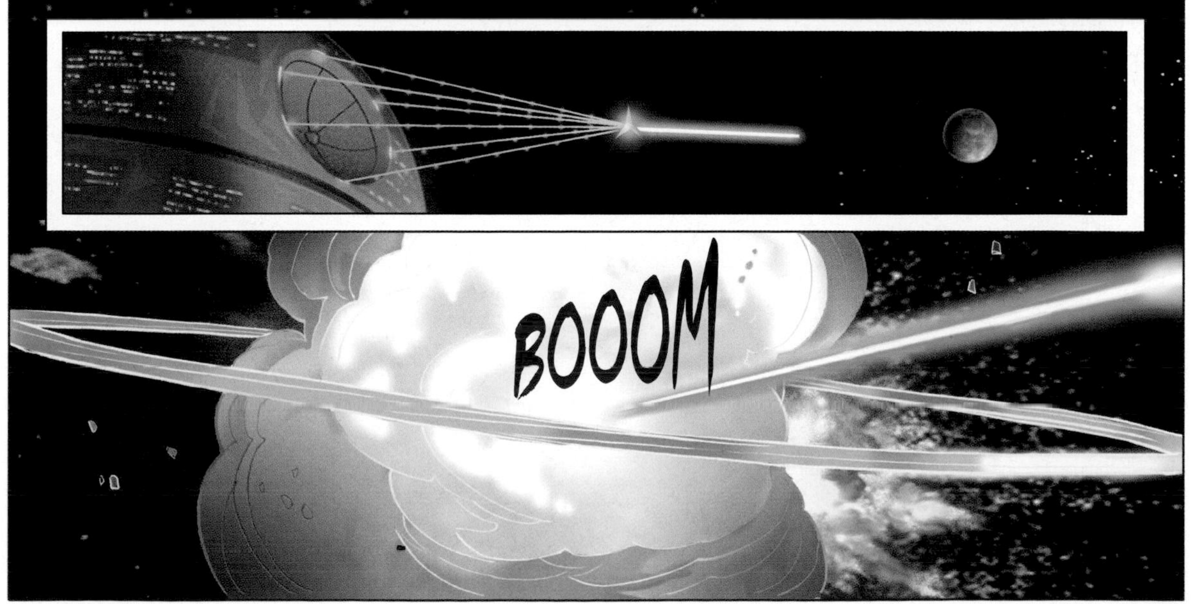
BOOOM

AT THE SAME TIME, ON THE MILLENNIUM FALCON...
!
WHAT'S WRONG?

I FELT A GREAT DISTURBANCE IN THE FORCE... AS IF MILLIONS OF VOICES CRIED OUT IN TERROR AND WERE SUDDENLY SILENCED.

I FEAR SOMETHING TERRIBLE HAS HAPPENED.

YOU'D BETTER GET ON WITH YOUR EXERCISES.
THIS TIME, LET GO OF YOUR CONSCIOUS SELF AND ACT ON INSTINCT.

WITH THE BLAST SHIELD DOWN I CAN'T EVEN SEE!

YOUR EYES CAN DECEIVE YOU. DON'T TRUST THEM.

ZMMM

FFHEW

FFHEW

YOU SEE, YOU CAN DO IT.
I CALL IT *LUCK.*

IN MY EXPERIENCE THERE IS NO SUCH THING AS LUCK.

YOU KNOW, I DID FEEL *SOMETHING.* I COULD ALMOST SEE THE REMOTE.
THAT'S GOOD. YOU'VE TAKEN YOUR FIRST STEP INTO A LARGER WORLD.

DEATH STAR. CONFERENCE ROOM.
OUR SCOUT SHIPS HAVE REACHED DANTOOINE. THEY FOUND THE ***REMAINS*** OF A REBEL BASE, BUT IT HAS BEEN DESERTED FOR SOME TIME.

SHE LIED! SHE ***LIED*** TO US!
I TOLD YOU SHE WOULD NEVER CONSCIOUSLY BETRAY THE REBELLION.

TERMINATE HER... IMMEDIATELY!

ALDERAAN SYSTEM.
WE'VE COME OUT OF HYPERSPACE INTO A ***METEOR SHOWER!***
WHAT'S GOING ON?
OUR POSITION IS CORRECT, EXCEPT... NO ALDERAAN!

AN IMPERIAL FIGHTER!

A FIGHTER THAT SIZE COULDN'T GET THIS DEEP INTO SPACE ON ITS OWN.

HE'S HEADING FOR THAT SMALL ***MOON!***

THAT'S NO MOON. TURN THE SHIP AROUND.

WE'RE CAUGHT IN A ***TRACTOR BEAM!*** THERE'S NOTHIN' I CAN DO ABOUT IT!

WE'VE CAPTURED A FREIGHTER. ITS MARKINGS MATCH THOSE OF A SHIP THAT BLASTED ITS WAY OUT OF MOS EISLEY.
THEY MUST BE TRYING TO RETURN THE STOLEN PLANS TO THE PRINCESS.

THERE'S NO ONE ON BOARD SIR.

SEND A ***SCANNING CREW*** ON BOARD. I WANT EVERY PART OF THIS SHIP CHECKED.

I SENSE SOMETHING... A ***PRESENCE*** I HAVEN'T FELT SINCE...

EVEN IF I COULD TAKE OFF, I'D NEVER GET PAST THE TRACTOR BEAM.
LEAVE THAT TO ME.

?
HEY DOWN THERE, COULD YOU GIVE US A HAND?

PEW
PEW

FORWARD BAY, COMMAND OFFICE.
FSHHHH

HROOOO!

PEW

WE FOUND THE COMPUTER OUTLET, SIR.

THE TRACTOR BEAM IS COUPLED TO THE MAIN REACTOR IN SEVEN LOCATIONS.
A POWER LOSS AT ONE OF THE TERMINALS WILL ALLOW THE SHIP TO LEAVE.

I DON'T THINK YOU BOYS CAN HELP. I MUST GO ALONE.

FSHHHH
I WANT TO GO WITH YOU.

YOUR DESTINY LIES ALONG A DIFFERENT PATH FROM MINE. THE FORCE WILL BE WITH YOU... ALWAYS!

○●●!
WHAT IS IT?

PRINCESS LEIA.
THE PRINCESS? SHE'S HERE? WHERE?
DETENTION BLOCK AA-23. I'M AFRAID SHE'S SCHEDULED TO BE *TERMINATED.*

OH NO! WE'VE GOTTA DO SOMETHING!
WHAT ARE YOU TALKING ABOUT? I'M NOT GOING ANYWHERE.

BUT THEY'RE GOING TO *KILL* HER!
BETTER *HER* THAN *ME.*

SHE'S RICH, POWERFUL! LISTEN, IF YOU WERE TO RESCUE HER, THE REWARD WOULD BE...
WHAT?

WELL, MORE *WEALTH* THAN YOU CAN IMAGINE!
I DON'T KNOW, I CAN IMAGINE QUITE A BIT.

SHORTLY AFTER...
THIS IS NOT GONNA WORK.
WHY DIDN'T YOU SAY SO BEFORE?
I DID SAY SO BEFORE!

DEATH STAR. DETENTION SECURITY AREA.
WHERE ARE YOU TAKING THIS... THING?
PRISONER TRANSFER FROM CELLBLOCK 1138.

I WASN'T NOTIFIED. I'LL HAVE TO CLEAR IT.

HROOOO!

PEW
PEW
PEW

PEW
PEW
PEW

WE GOTTA FIND OUT WHICH CELL THIS PRINCESS OF YOURS IS IN.
HERE IT IS... CELL 2187!

FSHHHHH

I'M LUKE SKYWALKER, I'M HERE TO *RESCUE* YOU!

CAN'T GET OUT THAT WAY!
LOOKS LIKE YOU MANAGED TO *CUT OFF* OUR ONLY ESCAPE ROUTE.

PEW
MAYBE YOU'D LIKE IT BACK IN YOUR CELL, YOUR HIGHNESS.
PEW

THIS IS SOME RESCUE.

WHAT ARE YOU DOING?

FLYOOOM

SOMEBODY HAS TO SAVE OUR SKINS.

PEW

PEW

INTO THE *GARBAGE CHUTE*, FLYBOY!

PEW

PEW

WONDERFUL GIRL! EITHER I'M GONNA *KILL* HER OR I'M BEGINNING TO *LIKE* HER!

"GET IN THERE, LUKE!"

OH! THE GARBAGE CHUTE WAS A REALLY WONDERFUL IDEA. WHAT AN INCREDIBLE SMELL YOU'VE DISCOVERED!

IT COULD BE WORSE.

THREEPIO! SHUT DOWN ALL THE GARBAGE MASHERS ON THE DETENTION LEVEL!
ARE YOU THERE, SIR?

SHUT DOWN ALL THE GARBAGE MASHERS ON THE DETENTION LEVEL!
SHUT THEM ALL DOWN! HURRY!

KRRR

VRRR
BEEP

ZLANK
!

AHAHAHA!
LISTEN TO THEM! THEY'RE *DYING*, ARTOO! CURSE MY METAL BODY, I WASN'T FAST ENOUGH!

THREEPIO! WE'RE *ALL RIGHT!* YOU DID GREAT!

I'VE BEEN WAITING FOR YOU, OBI-WAN.

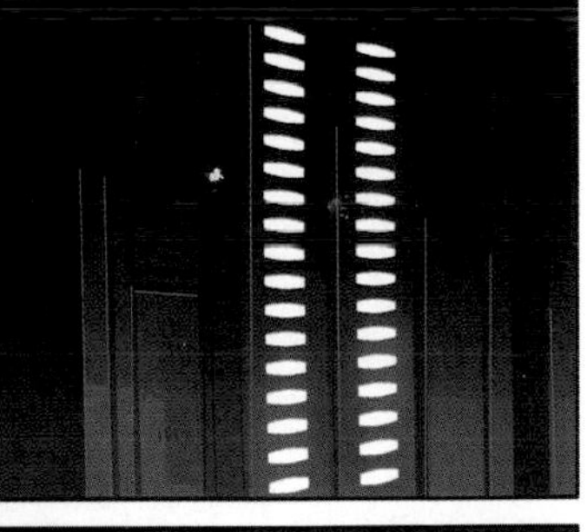

THE CIRCLE IS NOW *COMPLETE*. WHEN I LEFT YOU, I WAS BUT THE STUDENT... NOW I AM THE MASTER.
ZMM

ONLY A MASTER OF *EVIL*, DARTH.
SHZZ

IF WE CAN JUST AVOID ANY MORE FEMALE ADVICE, WE OUGHT TO BE ABLE TO GET OUT OF HERE.
LISTEN. I DON'T KNOW WHO YOU ARE OR WHERE YOU COME FROM, BUT FROM NOW ON, YOU DO AS I TELL YOU. OKAY?

LOOK, *YOUR WORSHIPFULNESS...* I TAKE ORDERS FROM JUST ONE PERSON, ME!
IT'S A *WONDER* YOU'RE STILL ALIVE.

IT'S THEM! BLAST THEM!

GET BACK TO THE SHIP!
PEW
PEW

HE CERTAINLY HAS COURAGE.

SO, WHILE HAN SOLO AND CHEWBACCA CREATE A DIVERSION...

...LUKE AND LEIA GET ACROSS THE CENTRAL CORE SHAFT...

...OBI-WAN FACES DARTH VADER NEXT TO THE MAIN FORWARD BAY.
YOUR POWERS ARE *WEAK*, OLD MAN.
VZAK

YOU CAN'T WIN, DARTH.
SHZZ

KZZZCH
IF YOU STRIKE ME DOWN I SHALL BECOME *MORE POWERFUL* THAN YOU CAN POSSIBLY IMAGINE.

MAIN FORWARD BAY. SHORTLY AFTER.
IS THE SHIP ALL RIGHT?
SEEMS OKAY, IF WE CAN GET TO IT.
JUST HOPE THE OLD MAN GOT THE *TRACTOR BEAM* OUT OF COMMISSION.

BEN?
NOW! RUN!

VMMM

NO!

PEW

PEW

PEW

PEW

WHOOOOO

I CAN'T BELIEVE HE'S GONE...

THEY HAVE JUST MADE THE JUMP INTO HYPERSPACE.
YOU'RE SURE THE ***HOMING BEACON*** IS SECURE ABOARD THEIR SHIP?
I'M TAKING AN AWFUL RISK, VADER. THIS HAD BETTER WORK...

FOURTH MOON OF YAVIN. MASSASSI TEMPLE, SECRET REBEL BASE.

YOU MUST USE THE INFORMATION IN THIS R2 UNIT TO HELP PLAN THE *ATTACK.*

"IT IS OUR ONLY HOPE."

YAVIN SYSTEM.
WE ARE APPROACHING THE PLANET YAVIN.
THE REBEL BASE IS ON A MOON ON THE FAR SIDE. WE ARE PREPARING TO ORBIT THE PLANET.

THE APPROACH WILL NOT BE EASY. YOU ARE REQUIRED TO MANEUVER STRAIGHT DOWN THIS ***TRENCH*** AND SKIM THE SURFACE TO THIS POINT.

THE TARGET AREA IS ONLY ***TWO METERS*** WIDE. IT'S A SMALL THERMAL EXHAUST PORT, RIGHT BELOW THE MAIN PORT.

THE SHAFT LEADS DIRECTLY TO THE REACTOR SYSTEM. A PRECISE HIT WILL START A ***CHAIN REACTION*** WHICH SHOULD DESTROY THE STATION.

MAN YOUR SHIPS! AND ***MAY THE FORCE BE WITH YOU!***

SO... YOU GOT YOUR REWARD AND YOU'RE JUST *LEAVING* THEN?

THAT'S RIGHT. I GOT SOME OLD DEBTS I'VE GOTTA PAY OFF WITH THIS STUFF.
COME ON! THEY COULD USE A GOOD PILOT LIKE YOU, YOU'RE TURNING YOUR BACK ON THEM!
ATTACKING THAT BATTLE STATION AIN'T MY IDEA OF COURAGE. IT'S MORE LIKE *SUICIDE*.
ALL RIGHT. WELL, TAKE CARE OF YOURSELF, HAN... I GUESS THAT'S WHAT YOU'RE BEST AT, ISN'T IT?
HEY, LUKE...
...MAY THE FORCE BE WITH YOU!

HANG ON *TIGHT*, ARTOO, YOU'VE GOT TO COME BACK.
•••
YOU WOULDN'T WANT MY LIFE TO GET BORING, WOULD YOU?

LUKE, THE FORCE WILL BE WITH YOU.
OBI-WAN?

STAND-BY ALERT. DEATH STAR APPROACHING. ESTIMATED TIME TO FIRING RANGE, *15* MINUTES.

RED LEADER HERE. LOCK S-FOILS IN ATTACK POSITION.
HEAVY FIRE, BOSS! 23 DEGREES!
I SEE IT. STAY LOW.
BOOM

SQUAD LEADERS, ENEMY FIGHTERS COMING YOUR WAY.
HERE THEY COME!

HE'S ON ME TIGHT, I CAN'T SHAKE HIM!
THIS IS LUKE: I'LL BE RIGHT THERE.

THE REBEL BASE WILL BE IN FIRING RANGE IN 7 MINUTES.

GOLD LEADER TO RED LEADER. WE'RE STARTING OUR ATTACK RUN.
I'LL TAKE THEM MYSELF! COVER ME!
REBEL BASE, 1 MINUTE AND CLOSING.

BIGGS, WEDGE, LET'S CLOSE IT UP. WE'RE GOING IN FULL THROTTLE!
RIGHT WITH YOU, BOSS!

R2, TRY AND INCREASE THE POWER!

I'M HIT! I CAN'T STAY WITH YOU!

GET CLEAR, WEDGE! YOU CAN'T DO ANY MORE GOOD BACK THERE!

STAY ON THE LEADER.

!

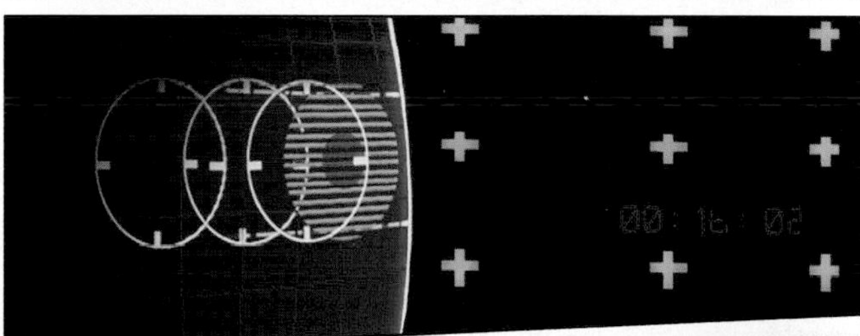

REBEL BASE, 30 SECONDS AND CLOSING.

BEEP
BEEP
BEEP

USE THE FORCE, LUKE.
LET GO, LUKE.

THE FORCE IS ***STRONG*** WITH THIS ONE*!*

LUKE, TRUST ME.

LUKE, YOU SWITCHED OFF YOUR TARGETING COMPUTER. WHAT'S WRONG?
NOTHING. I'M ALL RIGHT.

I'VE LOST ARTOO!

!
THE DEATH STAR HAS CLEARED THE PLANET
YOU MAY FIRE WHEN READY.
I HAVE YOU NOW.
WHAT?
YAHOO!

YOU'RE ALL CLEAR, KID.
"NOW LET'S BLOW THIS THING AND GO HOME!"

KA-BOOOM
ORR
GREAT SHOT, KID. THAT WAS ONE IN A MILLION!
REMEMBER, THE FORCE WILL BE WITH YOU... ALWAYS.

MASSASSI TEMPLE, MAIN THRONE ROOM. SOME TIME LATER...

•••

...THE REBELLION CELEBRATES ITS MOST IMPORTANT VICTORY!

THE END

"THE FORCE WILL BE WITH YOU, ALWAYS"

Obi-Wan Kenobi

CREDITS

Manuscript Adaptation
Alessandro Ferrari
Character Studies
Igor Chimisso
Layout and Clean Up
Matteo Piana
Ink
Alessandro Pastrovicchio, Matteo Piana
Paint (background and settings)
Davide Turotti
Paint (characters)
Kawaii Creative Studio
Special Thanks to
Michael Siglain, Jennifer Heddle,
Rayne Roberts, Pablo Hidalgo,
Leland Chee

Adapted from the film by George Lucas

Editorial Director
Bianca Coletti
Editorial Team
Guido Frazzini *(Director, Comics)*
Stefano Ambrosio *(Executive Editor, New IP)*
Carlotta Quattrocolo *(Executive Editor, Franchise)*
Camilla Vedove *(Senior Manager, Editorial Development)*
Behnoosh Khalili *(Senior Editor)*
Julie Dorris *(Senior Editor)*
Design
Enrico Soave *(Senior Designer)*
Cover Artist
Eric Jones
Editors
Justin Eisinger and Alonzo Simon
Collection Design
Clyde Grapa
Publisher
Greg Goldstein
Art
Ken Shue *(VP, Global Art)*
Roberto Santillo *(Creative Director)*
Marco Ghiglione *(Creative Manager)*
Stefano Attardi *(Computer Art Designer)*
Portfolio Management
Olivia Ciancarelli *(Director)*
Editing - Graphic Design
Absink, Edizioni BD, Lito milano S.r.l.
Contributors
Carlo Resca

For international rights, contact **licensing@idwpublishing.com**

ISBN: 978-1-68405-380-3 21 20 19 18 1 2 3 4

IDW®
www.IDWPUBLISHING.com

Facebook: facebook.com/idwpublishing • Twitter: @idwpublishing
YouTube: youtube.com/idwpublishing • Tumblr: tumblr.idwpublishing.com
Instagram: instagram.com/idwpublishing

Greg Goldstein, President & Publisher • **John Barber**, Editor-in-Chief • **Robbie Robbins**, EVP/Sr. Graphic Artist • **Cara Morrison**, Chief Financial Officer **Matthew Ruzicka**, Chief Financial Officer • **Anita Frazier**, SVP of Sales and Marketing • **David Hedgecock**, Associate Publisher • **Jerry Bennington**, VP of New Product Development • **Lorelei Bunjes**, VP of Digital Services • **Justin Eisinger**, Editorial Director, Graphic Novels and Collections • **Eric Moss**, Senior Director, Licensing and Business Development
Ted Adams, Founder and CEO of IDW Media Holdings